D0327987

THE LOVE TRIALS

BOOK TWO

J.S. COOPER & HELEN COOPER

THE LOVE TRIALS

BOOK TWO

PROLOGUE

A wise man once said that there are three sides to every story. His side. Her side. And the truth. The truth can set you free, but it can also set off a ticking bomb.

When it comes to love and sex, the truth can be a dangerous thing. Sometimes, it can cost you everything.

CHAPTER ONE

Jaxon

Women don't understand that men love the thrill of the chase. It sets something off in us. It is our instinct to pursue. Being pursued scares us away like a bunny rabbit seeing a fox crossing the yard on a hot summer day. I'm a wolf, a predator. I'm very patient in seeking my prey, and when I find her, I go in for the kill.

CHAPTER TWO

Nancy

I'm not usually impetuous. In fact, I'm not usually argumentative or feisty in any way. I'm the girl who keeps things inside. That nearly changed as I listened to Jaxon and his father talking. My first reaction was hurt. Then it turned quickly to shock, and then I became incensed with anger. Jaxon was playing me? He was trying to get me to fall for him? That's what it sounded like. The only question I had was why? Was this a game to him and his father?

I wanted to go and approach them both. I wanted to scream and about. I wanted to hit Jaxon in the chest and tell him what an asshole I thought he was. I wanted to do all of those things, but I didn't. There's something to be said for calmness. I had the ability to stay calm in almost all situations. I wasn't prone to outbursts and showing my emotions. In calmness, I could listen to reason and rationale. My own reason and rationale.

I knew that it was unlikely that Jaxon and his father would tell me the truth if I confronted them. They were playing a game with me. They had been from the train. I just needed to figure out if I'd become a target on the train or beforehand. If I'd become a target on the train, it meant that this was a smaller case of cat and mouse. If before the train, it meant something else entirely.

Quickly and quietly, I walked back to my room, thinking back to my time at the private club. I'd gone to the private club to find out the truth about my sister, Maria, and her death. By the time my ordeal was over, I'd found out that she was actually my mother. There had been so much going on under the surface of the private club, and I was beginning to wonder if that was the same thing here. What exactly was going on at the Lovers' Academy? Why was Jaxon teaching me? What did they get from this business?

I sat on the bed and hugged my pillow to me. I couldn't figure it out. At all. I knew that I needed help, and my mind immediately went to Meg. She would know what to do. She would be able to figure out the secrets. I knew she could do it better than I could. She'd put her heart on the line and won. I didn't think I had the same verve as her.

I was already confused. I'd come here for one guy who didn't even seem to remember me. I was thinking about sleeping with another guy who was somehow targeting me, yet here I still remained, even though I knew my dad would flip a switch if he knew where I was. My heart beat fast as I imagined his face when he found out that I had lied to him. He would be furious. Katie would have to take Harry and hide out because I was pretty sure he would give me the shouting match of my life. He hadn't known he was my dad for very long, but he had taken to the role easily and quickly.

My mind was buzzing as I lay in the bed. I couldn't stop thinking about Jaxon and his father talking, and I couldn't stop thinking about being in Jaxon's bed. His fingers and hands on me, touching me and teasing me. It made me squirm to remember just how badly I'd wanted him. Just how badly I still wanted him. I was ashamed of myself for wanting him still. I was ashamed that my body still craved him. I wanted to go back to his room. I wanted to beg him to touch me and finish what he had started. I froze as I realized that was his plan. He wanted me to want him. I hadn't known that sexual attraction could feel like this. It was mind numbing. And I hated him for making me feel this way.

I jumped up in my bed again. I needed to talk to Jaxon. I didn't care if he lied to me. I needed to tell him what I'd heard. I needed to see his reaction. I needed to know why he and his dad were talking about me.

I paused by the door as it suddenly hit me. What if they hadn't been talking about me? What if I had confused myself? What if there was someone else they had been targeting on the train? Shannon and Amber had been on the train as well. What if Jaxon and his father had been talking about them?

I slowly walked back to my bed, not feeling as confident anymore. I didn't want to confront him if I wasn't one hundred percent sure. I knew better than that. Then I remembered that I'd heard my name. I sighed as I realized that it was as bad as I had thought.

I drifted off to sleep at about two a.m. My mind was still thinking, but my body was exhausted. I wasn't surprised when I woke up at five a.m. feeling anxious and alone. I wanted to go home and forget everything, but a part of me knew that I couldn't. Not until I figured out what was going on here.

I jumped out of bed, not thinking about anything but getting the truth. I'd kept quiet in the private club and I'd nearly cost people their lives. I wasn't going to allow fear to stop me now. I knew I had to approach Jaxon. I had to be honest about what I'd seen and heard. I had to demand the truth. I knew that I wasn't a great sleuth. I was too trusting and I didn't have the killer instinct to do whatever. At my core, I was a scaredy cat. I'd rather crawl into bed and hide than face intruders. But this was something different. This was something I knew I couldn't let slide. I needed to know exactly what was going on with Jaxon and his dad. I quickly walked out of the bedroom door and headed to Jaxon's room.

"It's going to be fine," I muttered to myself as I walked briskly through the dark and quiet hallways. I was about to round the corner when someone grabbed me. "Argh!" I cried out.

"Be quiet, Nancy," a voice whispered in my ear, and I froze.

"Hunter?" I blinked rapidly and looked behind me. "Hunter, it's you."

"Yes." He gave me a half-smile. "It's me."

"You know me?" I was confused.

"Of course I know you." He gave me a wry smile. "Who could forget your beautiful face?"

My eyes widened. "Beautiful?"

"I suppose you're wondering what's going on?" he whispered and looked around the hallways.

"You could say that." I nodded, my heart racing. Hunter remembered me! I was ecstatic. He thought I had a beautiful face.

"We can't talk here." His fingers tightened around my waist.

"Where should we talk?"

"We can go back to my room." He looked down into my eyes and I could see a small glimpse of lust in his gaze that made me slightly uncomfortable.

"Is that a good idea?" I whispered slowly. "What if Shannon walks in and comes to find you?"

"Don't you want to know why I pretended like I didn't know you?"

"I do want to know." I nodded slowly, my mind going to Jaxon. I was starting to lose my resolve. "Can we talk later? There's something I need to do."

"What's that?" His fingers ran down my back, and I took a step back.

"I need to ask the owner some questions."

He frowned. "What owner?"

"Jaxon. I need to talk to Jaxon."

"Jaxon Cade?" He let go of my waist. "The guy you were with at the dinner?"

"Yeah." I nodded.

"He's not the owner." He laughed with a dark note in his tone.

"He's not?" I felt like my heart was slowly constricting and oxygen was hard to come by.

He looked into my eyes. "Why would you think he's the owner?"

"No reason." I shook my head slowly, all of a sudden feeling like I was in a really dark place.

The whole situation was starting to feel like déjà vu. I'd been in a situation like this before, where nothing had made sense and lies had been flowing. I hadn't liked it then and I sure as hell didn't like it now. I was angry and upset. Why had Jaxon told me he was the owner?

"So is Jaxon a teacher then?"

"A teacher? Jaxon?" Hunter raised an eyebrow. "I don't even think he likes women."

"He's gay?"

"Oh, I don't think he's gay." Hunter shrugged. "I just don't think he gives two shits about making sure a woman is a good lover."

"And you do?"

"That's why I'm a teacher."

"Why did you leave high school?"

"I don't want to talk about that now." He shook his head and grabbed my hand. "Come to my room with me."

"No, I can't." I pulled away from him. "I have a question for you. If Jaxon isn't a teacher or the owner, how do you know him?"

"His dad founded the school. Everyone knows him." His eyes bored into me. "They're big shots in this town."

"Oh?"

"Remember the train station stop?"

"Cadestown? So?" I paused and my eyes widened. "Oh! Cadestown as in Cade?"

"Yeah." Hunter's face looked bitter. "Must be nice to have a town named after you."

"So he's rich?" I asked stupidly, as if I didn't already know the answer to that.

"Why do you care?" Hunter looked jealous, and I felt my stomach flip in excitement. He really did like me.

"I don't care." I smiled up at him to console him. I wanted him to know that I liked him and that Jaxon was no threat.

"Why were you with him at dinner?" His eyes narrowed.

I felt something inside me twinge. I was starting to feel uncomfortable. I hadn't seen this side of Hunter before and I wasn't sure that I liked it.

"Because he was the first person I met and he asked me to sit with him." I felt annoyed inside and I wasn't sure why.

"Stay away from him." He pursed his lips. "He's not a good guy. I have no idea why he's paid any attention to you."

"Well, thanks." My face was heated.

"I'm not trying to be rude, Nancy." He leaned towards me. "Jaxon is bad news. As in really bad."

"What does that have to do with me?" I shivered.

"I don't know." His eyes bored into mine. "But he hasn't been here in months and he's certainly never paid attention to any of the women before."

"I think he..." I stopped. I wasn't sure why I was defending Jaxon. It wasn't as if I trusted him. "I want to know what his story is as well."

"You want to know what his story is more than mine?" Hunter made a sad face.

"It's not like that." I sighed, not liking how Hunter was trying to manipulate me.

"Tell me, Nancy. Why did you come here?" Hunter's blue eyes were bright with mischief. "Is it because you wanted to be seduced by me and made love to?"

"I came to get to know you better." I wasn't sure how to feel about his overtly sexual gaze.

"I was shocked when I saw you," he smiled and touched my hair. "At first, I wasn't sure what to do."

"Why didn't you just say hello?"

"I couldn't believe that all my fantasies were coming true."

"You had a fantasy about me?" I gasped, shocked. This was proof that he'd had a thing for me as well.

"You were the sexiest girl in Spanish class." His eyes darkened. "I'm not supposed to say this, but I always wanted to keep you back in class so that I could have my wicked way with you."

"Oh?" I smiled back at him, my heart racing.

The only problem I had with his comment was that I hadn't been in his Spanish class. I tried to ignore the disappointment at his words. If he really remembered me and had a crush on me, wouldn't he have known what classes of his I'd taken?

"Oh, Nancy Hastings, I've always had a thing for you." He leaned forward to kiss me, but a noise made me jump back.

"What's going on here?" A deep, dark voice walked towards us.

I looked up and saw Jaxon glaring at me. His eyes looked murderous and I could tell that he was furious.

"Nancy and I were just talking." Hunter shrugged and smiled at me, his hand still around my waist.

"I think it's time for you to go back to your room, Hunter." Jaxon's face was grim.

"I don't think so." Hunter looked at him. "I'm talking to Nancy."

"It's time for you to leave." Jaxon stopped in front of us, and I watched as his lips curled up in derision as he stared Hunter down.

I swallowed hard, trying not to stare at Jaxon's bare chest. I shivered as his eyes turned towards me. They were cold, and I could feel his gaze searching deep into my soul. I shivered as I stared at his clenched fists.

I spoke up. "Jaxon, we were just talking."

His eyes narrowed. "Was this planned?"

"That's not really any of your business, is it?" I raised an eyebrow at him.

"Everything you do is my business."

"Why is that?" I took a step towards him and looked up at him, searching for the truth in his eyes.

"You don't think he's going to tell you the truth, do you, Nancy?" Hunter touched my back, and I looked back at him, his familiar face looking older and harder than I remembered.

"What's that supposed to mean?" Jaxon grabbed me and pulled me to the side if him, laying his claim on me.

"I know you told Nancy you own the club." Hunter laughed. "Does your dad know that?"

"My dad?" Jaxon's voice rose, and I was sure he was about to punch Hunter, but he surprised me by smiling. "I see," he said finally, and there was a grim smile on his face.

"What do you see?" Hunter asked after a few moments of silence.

Jaxon ignored Hunter and looked over at me. His eyes looked me over slowly, and I felt my blood pressure rising at his intimate gaze. In that moment, all I could think about was him and his touch. I could still feel his tongue on me. I could still feel his hardness beneath me. I could feel his fingertips and the feather running across my skin. My head started feeling hazy as he continued staring at me. My blood was heating up, and I wanted to reach out and touch his chest. All I could think about was him and being consumed by him.

"Don't confuse sex with love, Nancy." Hunter's voice interrupted the moment and I looked away from Jaxon and stared at Hunter. There was a light in his eyes that I'd never seen before. It made my stomach jump. "There's a stark difference between love and sex. Just as there's a stark difference between good and evil. Remember why you came here." Hunter paused, and I watched as he ran his fingers through his hair. "I'll speak to you later." He nodded at me before walked down the hallway.

"Did you come to meet him on purpose?" Jaxon's voice was angry.

"Wasn't the point of you being my teacher to help me get Hunter? Shouldn't you be happy that it's already working?" I shrugged and saw Jaxon's lips thin as his eyes narrowed.

"Did you want to fuck him?"

"That's none of your business."

"Did you want him to touch you?"

"No!" I exclaimed angrily, and he smiled a slow, wide smile.

"Good." He reached out to touch me, but I took a step back.

"I don't want you to touch me either." My voice rose and I glared at him. "I don't know what game you're playing, Jaxon Cade, but I want to know the truth. I want to know why I'm at the Lovers' Academy, and don't tell me it's because you want to teach me how to seduce men. We both know that's not true."

"What if it's because I want you to seduce me?" His eyes fell to my breasts.

"Don't play games with me." I stood my ground and tried to ignore the tingling in my nipples.

"I want to do more than play games with you. I want to take you to my room, flip you onto your stomach, and enter you hard and fast." He stared into my eyes unblinking.

"I can't think of anything I want less," I lied and then yawned.

His eyes widened in anger and then he paused. "You want to play this game, Nancy?"

"I just want the truth." I reached out and touched his chest before reaching up and whispering against his lips, "My body is off-limits to you, Jaxon. I want no part of you. All I want is the truth." And with that, I turned around and hurriedly walked back to my room.

This wasn't the time for me to confront Jaxon about what I'd heard. I was out of sorts and my breathing was fast. My body felt weak and achy, and I knew that it would only take one touch before I was pressed up against him, begging him to give me the orgasm my body desired.

I hurried to my room and fell onto my bed as soon as I entered. I closed my eyes and Hunter's face entered my mind. His blue eyes were so bright and pure. I was shocked that he now knew who he was. Part of me was excited, but another part of me was distrusting. Something seemed off with him as well, and I didn't know what. He was as handsome as I remembered, but there was something about his demeanor that was harder than I remembered.

Then my head started ringing.

Hunter had called me Nancy Hastings. I hadn't been Nancy Hastings at the school. How did he know my name?

CHAPTER THREE

Jaxon

Nancy's trembling lips infuriated me as she told me that she didn't want me. All I wanted to do was touch her and watch her eyes fluttering as I teased her. I was pissed that she would dare to defy me. When I'd seen her with Hunter, I had felt something I'd never felt before and it annoyed me. And now, watching her walking away from me with fire in her step, I felt both aggravated me and turned on.

Nancy was a stupid girl with no common sense. I was angry at her. I'd met foolish women before, but she had absolutely no common sense and no protective instincts. The fact that she'd been cozied up with Hunter in the hallway told me that. I had no idea what his game was, but I had a feeling that I knew what was going on. My only decision was whether I was going to let Nancy go down that road.

My number-one rule was to never let a woman affect me in any way. If I thought they were getting too close, I backed away. I wasn't looking for any hassle. I'd never had to worry about getting too close to them. It had never happened. I didn't think it was possible. I'd never been in love.

I also never let a woman get close enough to affect my own decisions. My life would only become complicated if I let a woman in. I didn't even want to let Nancy in. I didn't want to care that she was on a path to hell. A path that had been set in motion by me. A path that was to be the ultimate revenge. I didn't want to feel like this—with this half regret and doubt.

I just needed to fuck her. I needed her to relent to me completely. Once I had her, she'd be out of my system and then I wouldn't care what happened to her. She was nothing to me, and I wasn't going to let her big brown eyes make me think anything else.

CHAPTER FOUR

Nancy

"I'm here to talk to you." I practiced knocking on his door and walking into his room. "Jaxon, I'm here to talk to you." I stared at myself in the mirror with a stern face. "Don't touch me. I don't want to sleep with you." I stared at my reflection and sighed. Even I wasn't fooling myself. I wasn't sure why I was so attracted to Jaxon, even knowing that he was a shady liar. "I'm here to talk," I started again and frowned. "Tell me the truth." I glared into the mirror.

"Who are you talking to?" Amber walked into my room, with Shannon following close behind her.

"Good morning to you both as well." I turned around and gave them both a quick smile.

"So, do tell about your hottie of a teacher." Amber jumped on the bed and grinned at me. "Spill all the details."

"Amber." Shannon made a face and rolled her eyes.

"Don't even pretend like you weren't just agreeing that he's hot as fuck." Amber raised an eyebrow at her. "Shit, he could fuck me and—"

"Amber." I put my hand up and stopped her. "Really?"

"Really." She laughed and lay back. "So have you fucked him yet?"

"Of course not!" I exclaimed in an appalled tone. There was no need for her to know just how close we'd come.

"Waste." She shook her head. "If he were my teacher, my clothes would have fallen off within five minutes and I would have slipped and fallen on top of his dick."

"Well, that's a pity he's not your teacher then," I snapped, starting to get annoyed at Amber's comments. "How is your teacher?"

"Keenan's a chump." She made a face.

"Oh?"

"He says I'm too aggressive." She sat up. "I told him he was lucky that I was willing to suck his cock when he didn't manscape."

"Manscape?"

"His balls are hairy. He needs to shave and make it clean and smooth. I'm not down for the fuzz. I want smooth. I bet Jaxon is hung and smooth." She sighed and then winked at me.

"I wouldn't know." I shrugged.

"Let me know when you find out. I'm thinking he's about eight inches. Hmm hmm, good." She wriggled in my bed, and I looked at Shannon, who was standing there, looking embarrassed as hell.

"So how's it going with, Hunter?" I asked Shannon softly, and she blushed.

"Fine." She bit her lower lip and looked away from me.

"You can tell me. It's fine." I gave her a reassuring smile. Now that I knew Hunter remembered and wanted me, I wasn't as worried that he was with Shannon.

"Oh. Well, we haven't done anything. He said he wants to work on my self-confidence first. He said if I don't have confidence, I can never be a seductress."

"Oh, sure. That makes sense." I smiled to myself. I was confident that Hunter was just telling her that because he didn't want to cheat on me.

I felt my stomach turning slightly as I realized that I'd already cheated on him. But it wasn't like we were committed. He'd pretended like he didn't even know me. I froze for a second as I realized that I might still have gone ahead with Jaxon even if Hunter had known me. There was something about Jaxon that was hard to resist. I wasn't sure what that said about me and my feelings for Hunter.

"He's cute. I see why you like him," Shannon spoke softly, and I could see a faint red blush on her face.

"Do you like him?" I leaned forward to more clearly look at her face.

"I don't know him." She looked away from me in a telling manner.

I didn't know what to say. Part of me wanted to tell her that I didn't mind, but I wasn't sure where that was coming from. Of course I minded. Hunter was supposed to be mine. I didn't want anyone else taking him away from me.

Amber spoke up. "Maybe you two can swap teachers. And then I can swap with Shannon. Shit, if I could have Jaxon in my bed, I'd be dropping it like it's hot."

"What?" I looked at her, barely able to hide my annoyance.

She jumped up off of the bed and started dancing and bending over to the ground. I watched as she moved her butt up and down and then looked at Shannon.

"Amber thinks she's a rap video queen." Shannon gave me a half-smile, and I laughed.

We both watched Amber dancing to the rap song in her head, and I wondered if she wasn't a bit crazy.

"Guys like it when you drop it like it's hot." Amber jumped back up and slapped her ass. "Show's them what you're working with."

"I see." I gave her a weak smile.

"Don't you believe me?" Amber looked down at me ass and laughed. "I guess you've got a flat ass, so you wouldn't know."

"I don't have a flat ass." I frowned.

"Well, you're not accentuating anything else." She gave me a superior look. "A guy likes to know that you can back that ass up good."

"Another rap song." Shannon rolled her eyes.

"Oh." I grinned. "I guess I need to listen to more rap."

Amber's eyes lit up. "We should all go to a club."

"Why don't you work on that?" I sighed. "I've got something to do."

All of a sudden, nerves hit me again. I was worried and anxious to go and talk to Jaxon. I wanted to know the truth, but I was scared. I was scared that he wasn't going to tell me the truth, and I was scared that he was going to tell me. All of a sudden, I wished that I were back home, playing with Harry and talking to Meg and Katie about the wedding.

"Are you kicking us out?" Amber looked annoyed, and I smiled to myself.

I was pretty sure that Amber had thought she was the alpha dog among us girls. And maybe she could boss Shannon around and do what she wanted, but I wasn't as silent as I looked. And I sure wasn't a pushover. Not anymore.

"Sorry, girls. Don't mean to be rude, but we'll catch up later."

"Come on, Shannon. Let's go where we're wanted." Amber tossed her hair and headed towards the door. "We'll see you later, Nancy."

"See you girls." I smiled at Shannon as she left the room and grinned at myself in the mirror as soon as they'd exited my room. Score one for me.

I was finally being authoritative and sticking up for myself. I only hoped that I wouldn't crumble as soon as I came into contact with Jaxon.

***

I quickly walked out of my room and hurried to Jaxon's room before I could think about what I was doing. I didn't want to give myself any opportunity to back down or freak out over my confrontation. I didn't even bother to knock on his door before I entered, though that was based on principle. He never knocked on my door, so why should I knock on his?

"I want to talk to you." I pulled my cardigan across my chest and folded my arms as I walked into his room.

"Talk." He looked at me, unblinking, his face blank.

This wasn't what I'd expected. He wasn't giving me 'I want to fuck you' eyes or trying to touch me. He wasn't asking me why I had just barged into his room without knocking,

"I came back to your room last night," I started, but he didn't say anything. "I saw you and your dad talking." His eyes flashed briefly, but still he didn't say anything. "I heard you as well." I paused and rounded my shoulders. "And I want to know what the fuck is going on?" My voice rose as I grew angry at his lack of response.

His lips twitched then.

I frowned at him. "This is no laughing matter."

"What the fuck is going on?" He smirked as he finally spoke and repeated my words.

I got straight to the point. "Did you target me on the train or did you know who I was before the train?"

"Target you for what?" He tilted his head to the side.

"You tell me." I pushed my fingers into his chest.

"Couldn't resist huh?" He took a step towards me.

"Resist what?" I swallowed hard as he took another step.

"Touching me." He grabbed my fingers and pulled me towards him. "You want me."

"I want to know what's going on." My breath caught as I felt his body next to mine, warm and hard.

I should have known he would try and use our chemistry to distract me from why I was here. His body was playing games with me and my brain was quickly forgetting to be angry and afraid.

"What's it worth to you?"

I blinked up at him. "What's what worth?"

"The truth."

"The truth?"

"About why you're here." His face darkened as his hands fell to my ass and pushed me into him.

"Of course I want to know the truth." I stared into his eyes, unflinching.

"How badly?" He shifted and I felt his bulge pressing into my stomach hard.

I refused to take the bait. "I want to know."

"If I tell you, you have to do something for me."

I bit my lower lip. "What?"

"You have to spend the day and night with me and do what I want."

"I'm not going to have sex with you."

"I never force anyone to have sex with me."

"Then what?"

"You'll see."

"I don't know." I shook my head. Could I really trust him?

"I'm not going to hurt you." His fingers ran down my arms. "Think of it as a part of your training."

"What training?" I frowned.

"How to please me."

"How to please you?" I looked up at him in surprise, and I could tell from the look on his face that he hadn't meant to say that.

"How to please a man," he corrected himself with a frown.

"How to please Hunter?" I smiled slowly, wanting to see his reaction.

"No." His eyes flashed and his fingers tightened on my arms.

"No what?"

"Hunter is not the one for you." He shook his head angrily. "Why are women always so dumb?"

"Are you calling me dumb?"

"You're not the first woman who has been young and dumb, and I'm pretty sure you won't be the last either."

"I'm not dumb."

"You're not very smart either."

"Stop changing the subject. This isn't about me and Hunter."

"Do you think Hunter would like to know you've been kissing me?" He grinned. "And touching me? And allowing me to touch you? What do you think he'd think about the lap dance you gave me?"

"I'm sure he'd laugh," I spoke slowly and licked my lips. "I'm sure he'd have been able to make me come."

"Bitch." Jaxon's eyes narrowed as he stared at me.

"Really?" It was my turn to tilt my head. "I thought bitches were allowed to come as well, or is that not allowed here?"

"You're feistier than first appearances led me to believe." He shook his head as he stared at me. "You've more fire than I thought."

"You shouldn't play with fire." I smiled. "You might get burned."

"Small fires shouldn't play with big fires." He leaned towards me and whispered against my lips, "A big fire can consume a small fire in seconds." His lips pressed gently against mine. "Before you know where you are, there's nothing left of the small fire."

"Maybe a small fire is ready to take that risk," I whispered back, allowing my tongue to lightly run across his lower lip. "No matter the size of the fire, you get too close, you're going to get burned."

"Are you saying you're going to burn me, Nancy?"

"Are you saying you're going to consume me, Jaxon?"

"I've already consumed you, Nancy. You just haven't realized it yet."

"What game are you playing?"

"Do we have a deal?" He grabbed my hand and pulled me over to the couch.

"Yes." I nodded, not caring what I was agreeing to. I needed to know the truth.

"You're not being targeted per se." His eyes stared at me with no emotions. "My father is after your dad."

"Brandon?" I frowned.

"Yes, my father is after Brandon Hastings." He nodded.

"Why?"

"Why else?" He shrugged. "Revenge."

"And he's using me to get it?"

"No, he's using me."

"How?"

"He's using me to use you."

"Why would you tell me this?"

"I don't want to use you." He shrugged. "Whatever I get from you has to be given of your own volition."

"You think I'm just going to let you do things to me after you've told me I'm here for revenge?" I jumped off the bed. "You're crazy."

"You promised me that we had a deal."

"I lied." I stared at him for a few seconds, not moving. "Why does your dad want revenge on Brandon?"

"I thought you were going to leave."

"If I were smart, I'd leave."

"So you're not smart?" His lips twitched.

"Maybe you're not smart. Why would you tell me why I were here?"

"Because I know you're not going to leave." He shrugged. "You're already too invested."

"I came for Hunter," I spat out, not wanting him to think that I was going to stay because of him. "And he knows me."

"Yes, he knows you." He nodded.

"I've never done this before." I took a deep breath. I was confused and overwhelmed. I hadn't expected Jaxon to be so up-front with me. I knew I should leave the academy and never come back, but I didn't want to.

"Neither have I."

"What do you mean?" I looked up at him in confusion.

"I've never seduced someone I like."

"You like me?" I ignored the seduced part of his sentence. I didn't want to think too closely about the lust running through my body.

"Don't let it go to your head." He frowned.

I grinned at him. "As if I would."

"Your lips are like fire." He jumped up, leaned forward, and kissed me.

"Because of my red lipstick?" I asked after kissing him back lightly. There was something so potent about kissing him.

"No."

"Then why?"

"Because when I kiss you, you burn right through to my soul."

My heart froze at his words. "What do you mean?"

"Your heat has my internal organs out of sorts."

"Maybe you do have a heart after all." I smiled at him gently. Maybe that was why he had told me. Maybe a part of him cared about me, even in this short amount of time.

"More like a hard-on."

I shook my head. "You're disgusting."

"And you love it." He grinned and leaned forward to kiss me again.

"Tell me why your dad wants revenge against Brandon."

"Your dad is a hypocrite and a cheat."

"Why?"

"How much do you know about you dad?" His eyes glossed over. "I understand you just recently met him."

"So you do know about my past?" I stepped back from him. "You did know me on the train."

"I knew you on the train." He nodded. "I knew you when you walked to the train station. I knew you when you received the letters."

"You're Mr. X?"

He nodded. "Disappointed?"

"I thought it was Hunter."

"I know."

"How?" I nibbled my lower lip and shivered. "This is really creepy. You're really creepy. You're a fucking stalker."

"You love *fucking*, don't you?"

"Excuse me?"

"You love to use the word fucking. Fucking this, fucking that."

"You'll never hear the words me fucking you though." I smiled at him sweetly, and he pulled me towards him roughly. My breasts crushed against his chest and my breath caught. "What are you doing?" I gasped as his hands roughly squeezed my ass.

"I'm waiting."

"For what?"

"For you to beg me," he whispered in my ear, and then I felt his teeth nibbling on my earlobe. "I've told you before, Nancy, but I'm going to tell you again. I'm going to love watching you beg me to fuck you."

CHAPTER FIVE

Jaxon

Nancy's mouth dropped open as I massaged her firm ass. She squirmed against me, and I had to stop myself from pushing her onto the ground and undoing my zipper. Sex would be the undoing of Nancy, just as it was with all women. I'd lulled her into a false sense of security by letting her know some of the truth. It was bound to come out at some point. Now that I'd proactively told her the truth, she would have some sense of trust towards me.

She'd be stupid to trust me—especially after I'd told her that my father was after revenge. Any smart person would have fled and not looked back. However, Nancy—like most women— had a false sense of confidence. I never understood why women trusted so easily, even when blatantly confronted with the truth. I couldn't name how many women I'd told that I wasn't looking for a relationship. How many times I'd said, "I don't love you." How many times I'd never called. Yet they always came back for more. Always expected something to be different. I didn't understand why women didn't believe men when we told them that we were wolves.

I'd give it to her; she had more spunk than I'd thought she have. She was sexier than I'd imagined as well. Even now, with my hands all over her, it wasn't enough. I wanted more of her. I needed more of her. Yet I knew that I didn't want to hurt her. I didn't want to be a casualty of what my father and I were going to do to her father. I was going to change the plan. I had to.

Though I think my father already knew. I was pretty confident that he'd already moved on to plan B. I shouldn't have told him that there was a complication. My father didn't have a heart. There were no complications in his life. He took care of them quickly. I was pretty sure he'd already moved on. He wasn't counting on me anymore. That made me angry for more than one reason. I wanted to bring Brandon Hastings down as much as he did. I just didn't want Nancy to get hurt.

I felt my head pounding as I realized that she'd already gotten to me. She was the first woman to ever make me think twice about what I was doing. She was already under my skin and I barely knew her.

I knew that I needed to scare her if I wanted to ensure that she didn't get hurt. I'd have to show her part of the real me. I'd have to take her down my road. I knew my father would expect it. He'd be watching and waiting. I knew that he wouldn't hesitate to change things up. He'd already gotten the ball rolling.

I felt my insides heating up as I thought about Nancy's conversation with Hunter. There was no way I was going to sit by and watch her with him. No way at all.

I looked into her eyes then and smiled at the defiant gaze on her face. I'd have fun with her, break out the ropes and the whips. Turn the kink up. See how far down the road she'd go. See how many games she'd play. See how far to the dark side I could take her before she finally gave in and relented. Then I'd let her go. Hopefully, by that time, we wouldn't be too far into the game that we both got lost.

CHAPTER SIX

Nancy

"I'm never going to want to sleep with you." I turned my nose up at Jaxon and ignored his smirk.

"Let's test that theory." He smiled and took a step towards me, his eyes staring into mine with such intensity that my body shivered at his gaze.

"It's not a theory. It's a fact."

"Is that true now?" He ran his fingers across his temple.

"Yes."

"I want you to take this phone." He reached into his pocket and handed me a phone.

"What's this for?"

"I want you to have a bath tonight." He stared at me. "I want you to call me from that phone right as you step into the bath."

"Why?" I frowned.

"You'll see."

"I'm not going to send you a naked video of myself."

"I don't want a naked video."

"What do you want then?"

"You'll see." He looked at his watch. "You can go now."

"What?"

"I've got things to do."

"What am I supposed to do?"

"Think about what I told you."

"I don't get it. If your father hates Brandon and he's trying to bring me down to hurt him, why should I trust you?"

"Because I trusted you." He shrugged. "I don't want to see you get hurt."

"Why not?" My breath caught. Did he like me?

"Because contrary to what you might believe, I don't like to see innocent people paying for the actions of their fathers."

"Scared what you might have to pay for, huh?"

"Smart girl." He gave me a short smile.

"So your father is shady, but you're not?"

"My father is a businessman and so am I." His eyes glittered at me.

I wondered what he was saying. Was he saying that he was as shady as his dad? And if so, how shady?

"I'm guessing you're not going to tell me about all of your businesses?" I sighed.

"Smart girl." He ran his fingers to my face.

"Tell me why your dad hates Brandon."

"He ruined my father's business." He shrugged.

"What do you mean?" I frowned.

"We'll talk later."

I shook my head. "I want to talk about this now."

"Trust me, Nancy." His fingers ran down my cheek. "I've already told you the most important part. Have some patience and trust me."

"Fine." I nodded and sighed. Jaxon had already told me more than I would have ever expected him to tell me.

"Just take the phone, go and relax, and call me when you go to have a bath." He leaned forward and kissed my forehead. "Trust me. You won't regret it."

***

"It's me," I spoke into the phone softly as I settled into the hot bath.

"Are you in the bath?" he whispered.

"Yes."

"Naked?"

"Of course."

"Good." His voice lowered. "Close your eyes."

"Why?" I frowned into the phone.

"Don't ask. Just do."

"You're rather bossy for someone so shady."

"You think I'm shady?"

"Is that even a question?" I retorted as I closed my eyes. I smiled as I listened to his hearty laugh.

"Are you lying back in the water?"

"That's what most people do in a bathtub," I mumbled as I submerged my body in the hot water. It tingled my skin, but it felt marvelous.

"Stop talking back and just relax."

"Yes, sir!"

"You like that, don't you? I think you've got a fetish for men in authority."

"Is that a joke?" I mumbled, Jaxon's handsome face popping into my mind.

"Well, first the teacher and then me."

"You have no authority over me."

"Wrong answer. You were supposed to say not Hunter."

"Not Hunter what?" I yawned, suddenly feeling tired.

"Nothing, Nancy." He sighed. "Stop yawning. It's not safe to fall asleep in the bath."

"You're the one who told me to have a bath."

"Cradle the phone in the nook of your neck," he whispered, his voice lower and deeper. Something about his tone sent a thrill of pleasure down my spine.

"Are you trying to seduce me in the bathtub?" I whispered as I shifted the phone and ran my fingers down the valley between my breasts.

"Do you want me to?" He was breathing into the phone.

"No." My voice sounded sharp as my fingers moved to my breasts. I ran my fingertips over my nipples, and my body shuddered as I imagined it was him touching me.

"I want you to touch yourself."

"What?" I exclaimed guiltily. Did he know that I was already doing that?

"I want you to touch yourself. There's no need to be shy."

"I'm not shy." I laughed slightly. If only he knew.

"What's so funny?" he questioned. I could tell from his tone that he was curious to know what was going on.

"Nothing's funny." I breathed into the phone and took a deep breath. I was starting to feel even more relaxed.

"I told you. Don't fall asleep on the phone."

"I'm not," I mumbled.

"Run your fingers down to your stomach."

"Why?"

"Don't question me again."

"Why why why?" I said quickly, and I heard him groan.

"Nancy, a woman who is comfortable in her own skin and sexuality can do anything. She has no fear."

"Oh." I paused and grinned. "I thought you were going to say a woman who can give herself an orgasm doesn't need to depend on men."

Jaxon laughed in response, his laughter growing deeper with every second that passed. "Do you get yourself off a lot then, Nancy?"

"That's none of your business, Jaxon."

"What happened to sir?"

"I wasn't sure if you'd prefer master," I quipped back, half joking.

"You wouldn't make a good sub. You're too mouthy."

"What, are you a Dom or something?" I shivered as I thought about the things he would command me to do if he was in that position over me. Part of me thought it could be extremely exciting.

"Touch yourself," was his answer to me, and I felt my nerves buzzing. Was he commanding me to let me know he was a Dom?

"Where?" I whispered back, caught up in the heat of the moment.

"Run your fingers between your legs." He paused. "Lean back, relax, and make sure your eyes are closed. Take a couple of deep breaths. Then run your fingers to your thighs. Don't touch your clit yet. Just run your fingers along your legs and through your pussy gently."

"And?" I whispered as my fingers gently ran over my pulsing skin.

"Just do that until I say."

"Okay," I whispered into the phone as I spread my legs wider in order to touch myself.

"Your fingers are soft and gentle," he muttered into the phone. "Imagine they are rough and hard. Imagine they graze you with the intent to tease, to torment."

Jaxon's image popped into my mind and I imagined him touching me. I imagined they were his fingers running across my labia and clit. I groaned as I started touching and rubbing myself.

"I hope you're not playing with yourself." His voice sounded angry.

"I'm not," I lied as I felt an orgasm building up.

"Whose face are you picturing in your mind as you play with yourself?" he asked me gently.

"Yours," I responded without thinking, so close to orgasm that my breathing was heavier and my fingers were working extra hard.

"Stop." His voice was low and deadly.

"What?" I froze as I heard a knock on the door.

"I said stop." His voice sounded louder on the phone, and my eyes popped open as the door opened.

"What are you doing?" I stared up at him in shock and excitement as he entered the bathroom.

"What are you doing?" He raised an eyebrow and stared at my flushed face and them down to my pussy. My finger was still next to my clit.

"Nothing." I flushed and moved my hand away.

"No." He smiled slowly and stood above me. His eyes ran down my naked body and darkened. "I want to see."

"See what?" I whispered, suddenly feeling modest but not covering up my breasts.

"I want to see you touch yourself." His lips curled upwards and he sat down on the toilet seat. "Yes, I'd like to see that very much."

"I don't—"

"Don't talk back." He leaned forward and grabbed my hand. Then he moved it down to my pussy and dropped it there.

I stared up at him with wide eyes. It had been one thing to play with myself while he was on the phone, but I didn't know that I could do it now that he was here in front of me.

"There's nothing to be ashamed of, Nancy."

"I'm not ashamed." I closed my eyes and lay back.

I gently ran my fingers back and forth and pretended I was by myself in my bed. I ran my fingers to my clit and rubbed softly and then hard. I gasped as the familiar feelings of pleasure swam through me. I lifted my legs to the sides of the bathtub and spread my legs wider. I was so close to orgasm—I could feel it. My hips started moving slightly in the water as my body got ready for the climax that was soon to come. And then I felt Jaxon's fingers on mine, moving my fingers faster, harder, rougher, increasing the intensity of pressure on my clit.

"Ooh!" I gasped as his fingers left mine. My eyes widened in disappointment as I realized that it was just me touching myself again. It was definitely less intense than when he'd been guiding me.

"Don't stop." He kneeled down next to the bathtub and ran his fingers across my nipples as I continued playing with myself. "Tell me when you're about to come."

His eyes bored into mine, and I nodded, suddenly overwhelmed by sensations. His fingers pinched my nipples hard, and I cried out and increased the pace of my fingers. My body began to quake, and my eyes flew to his.

"I'm about to come!" I exclaimed.

Jaxon's fingers immediately left my nipples and I felt them enter my pussy as I started to explode. His fingers fucked me as I continued to rub myself, and my juices poured out onto his hands and into the water. My body erupted in a heat of sexual lava, and my orgasm seemed to last forever.

Just when I thought I was done, Jaxon's fingers continued to work until another eruption hit me. This time, I had no control over my body, and I shook and squirmed as he brought me the most intense orgasm of my life. I lay in the water with my eyes closed for a few more seconds and then opened them slowly. Jaxon was staring at me with a smug smile on his face.

"Still think you do it better?" He raised an eyebrow and licked his lips.

"I never said that." I sat up in the bathtub and splashed water over my body.

"You'll never be satisfied playing with yourself now. You'll always wish I were there to help."

"You're full of yourself. Is that part of your revenge?"

"My revenge wouldn't have you orgasming."

"Are you going to tell me anything else?"

"Now's not the time to talk about this."

"I want to."

"You don't always get what you want."

I ignored him then. I was fed up of him treating me like some sort of kid. I was a woman and I had a right to know exactly what was going on. I didn't need him to hide anything from me.

"Are you ready for another lesson?" He pulled me up out of the bathtub.

"What's the lesson?" I asked as I shivered. I looked around for the towels but realized that Jaxon had one in his hands already.

"Don't be embarrassed." He pulled the towel around my body, and I clutched it to me.

"I'm not embarrassed," I lied smoothly. I was mortified.

I wasn't sure who I was around him. His fingers had been inside of me, taking me on a journey I'd never experienced before. It had been amazing and nerve racking.

"Your face is red and you're having trouble making eye contact with me." His fingers reached under my chin and he lifted my face up to look at him.

"I'm looking at you now."

"Who did you think about as you touched yourself?"

"Why do you care?"

"Who did you think about?"

"I don't remember." I shrugged, feeling slightly guilty that Hunter was not the one who had occupied my thoughts.

"Why did you come to the academy, Nancy? Aside from Hunter? Why did you come?" Jaxon questioned with a curious expression on his face as he rubbed me dry with the fluffy, white towel.

"I don't know." I thought for a moment. "Maybe I wanted to get away from home for a bit. Find out who I am." I sighed as I thought about the last few months.

"It's been a crazy time, huh?"

"You could say that." I gave him a small smile. "I found out that my sister gave me up to her parents after I was born. So my grandparents raised my as their own. Then I found out that her ex-boyfriend and boss is really my dad."

"That must have been hard."

"It was weird. I hated him when I thought he was my mom's ex-boyfriend, but as I realized he was my dad, the hate disappeared."

"Why do you think that happened?"

"A couple of reasons." I paused to think, and I stared at Jaxon for a few moments, not even sure why I was telling him this. It was something I hadn't even addressed to myself. "I think I always felt that something was missing on my life. And now I have Harry and Meg, and well, everything is fitting into place."

"Is Meg Brandon's new wife?"

"No, Katie is his fiancée. She's great as well, though I don't know her like I know Meg. Meg is Greyson's fiancée."

"Greyson Twining?" Jaxon looked surprised.

"You know him?"

"Everyone knows Greyson Twining." He nodded. "Brandon's worse half."

"Why do you say that?"

"Everyone knows that Greyson was the force behind the private club. We all know Brandon left and took over Hastings Enterprises."

"Do you hate Brandon or Greyson?"

"I don't care for either of them, but it's Brandon who took us under."

"What did he do?" I asked softly, wanting to know who my father really was and why so many people seemed to hate him.

"He invested in my father's company and then destroyed it. He deliberately destroyed it until he had nothing left but the Lovers' Academy."

"Why?" I frowned. "Why would he do that?"

"He wanted my father to close the Lovers' Academy."

"But he didn't?"

"That's all he has left." Jaxon sighed. "My father gave up everything to keep the academy."

"Why would Brandon want him to close it?"

"The same reason why he left the private club."

"Someone killed themselves here?"

"No one's died here." He shook his head. "Though I suppose that could solve a lot of problems."

"Then why?"

"Sex. Selling sex."

My eyes widened. "Is this a whorehouse?"

"Depends in your definition of a whorehouse. Do we train high-class escorts? Yes. Do we work for the johns? No."

"I don't get you. You're telling me that you train prostitutes?" I looked at him in disappointment.

"Not prostitutes. Escorts. There's a difference."

"What's the difference?"

"A few grand a night and no street corners." He grinned at me, but I didn't smile back.

"You're being serious here? You're training me to be a prostitute?"

"You're not going to be an escort, no." His eyes darkened.

"That was the plan though, wasn't it? To pimp me out?"

"Nancy." He grabbed my hand and led me back to the bedroom.

"Don't Nancy me! That was your dad's plan, right? To turn me into a working girl."

"Perhaps."

"So you're my pimp?"

"I'm not a pimp."

"Or should I call you my john?"

"It's okay for me to teach you about sex but not for you to be an escort? Don't you see something hypocritical there?"

"I didn't come to learn about sex or to be a ho." I tightened the towel around me as I sat on my bed.

"You came to be with Hunter." He frowned and pursed his lips at me.

"How did you even know to hire him?" I looked up at him in confusion. "Or was this some weird coincidence?"

"My dad has a friend named Frank."

"Frank!" I felt myself growing angry. If I'd only known how much my mother's ex-boyfriend had betrayed me. I was so angry that I'd trusted him for even a minute.

"He told us everything he knew about you."

"I guess you think you know my life story now."

"We knew about your crush on Hunter." He sighed. "So my father found Hunter and offered him a job."

"And then Frank told me where he worked," I said bitterly. "So I was set up."

"At least you've still got Hunter."

"Yeah." I sighed. "There's that."

"And you've got me as your teacher."

"My pimp. Yay. I have a pimp."

"You can leave if you want. I won't stop you." He sat next to me on the bed.

"Why are you telling me all of this?" I frowned. "And if I leave, what happens next?"

"If you leave, my dad will find another way to get revenge on your dad."

"So it's in my best interests to stay." I sighed.

"Well, Brandon's." He shrugged.

"My dad and my family are my life," I whispered. "I would never let anything happen to them."

"You have Hunter too."

"And you." I looked at him and saw him cringe at my comment. "I'm joking, Jaxon. I know I don't have you. I'm just grateful to you for telling me the truth."

"It's the least I could do."

"So what next? I go along and make your dad think you're training me?"

"Yeah." He nodded. "That's basically it for now."

"So when's our next lesson?" I took a deep breath.

"We can have one now."

"Oh?"

"The art of relaxation and letting go." He ran his fingers across my bare shoulders and I jumped.

"What are you doing?" I looked at him through lowered lashes.

"I want to teach you how to relax."

"I am relaxed."

"The tension in your shoulders tells me otherwise." His fingertips massaged me. "To be a confident woman and lover, you have to be relaxed and comfortable at all times."

"Okay."

"Lean back."

"Why?"

"Just do it."

"Uhm, you're moving a bit fast, aren't you? Revelation to lesson in 2.5 seconds."

"What would you prefer?"

"I wouldn't mind a revelation from you."

"What?" He frowned and pushed me back into the bed.

"If we're going to continue being intimate, I want to know more about you." I stared up at him and looked into his surprised eyes. I'd surprised myself as well. I really did want to know about him.

"What's there to know? I'm imperfectly perfect."

"Imperfectly perfect?" I reached up and touched his face. "I like that. I guess I'm perfectly imperfect."

"I'd say you're pretty perfect." He smiled and collapsed on the bed next to me.

"What are you doing?"

"Switching off for a second." He turned towards me. "It's tiring being me."

"You sound like you have the weight of the world on your shoulders." I stared at the lines in his face. "What do you do for a living?"

"A little bit of this and a bit of that. Business stuff mostly. Mainly stocks."

"Okay." I took a deep breath. "What about your love life?"

"What about it?" He frowned, and I stared at his handsome features so close to mine.

"Do you have a girlfriend?"

"You think I have a girlfriend?"

"I don't know."

"I was just fingering you." His hands ran across my collarbone.

"What?" I looked away from him and shifted my legs. I could feel myself growing wet at his words.

"If I had a girlfriend, I wouldn't have been fingering you. I wouldn't be lying here next to you, wanting to rip your towel off and bury my head in your pussy."

"I see."

"Do you really, Nancy?" His eyes glittered into mine.

"Do you say these outlandish things because you think you're shocking me?" I grinned at the look of surprise in his face. "You can't shock me, Jaxon. I went to public school. I just got out of a crazy stint at the private club. I might look demure and sweet, but I've got a backbone and it takes a lot to shock me."

"I don't know what to say." He looked searchingly in my eyes.

"Don't tell me. You don't know anyone quite like me."

"You took the words right out of my mouth." He shook his head.

"My best friend is kick-ass." I grinned at him. "I learned it all from her."

"Meg?"

"Yeah." I nodded. "I never had someone like her in my life before. Someone so feminine yet so fearless and kick-ass. She taught me that you do anything for friends and family. You do anything for love."

"Who are you doing this for? Your love of your family or your love of Hunter?" He held a hand up. "Actually, don't answer that. I'm not sure I want to know."

"What's your preoccupation with me and Hunter? Do you like him or not?"

"I don't care about him either way. If you haven't figured it out yet, I don't care much about others."

"Why not?"

"Maybe because my father is the male Mrs. Havisham."

"Great Expectations?"

"You read a lot?"

"A bit." I shrugged. "We did Dickens in AP English."

"You remind me of our age difference when you talk about AP anything." He groaned.

"What do you care?" I raised an eyebrow and laughed. I was starting to feel giddy while lying here, talking to Jaxon as if it were the most natural thing in the world.

"I guess I don't." He raised an eyebrow back at me, slowly reached down, and tugged on the knot at the top of my towel.

I felt it opening and falling off my body and to the bed. I lay there, staring at him confidently, not wanting him to know how badly I wanted to cover myself again. He reached over, and I felt his fingers lightly grazing my nipples.

"You've got beautiful breasts."

"Have you ever had a girlfriend?" I asked him softly, curious as to who this man was.

"Nope." He shook his head, his eyes darkening. "I don't lie to women."

"Have you never wanted a girlfriend?"

"I like sex and I get it without a title." He shrugged.

"You look so hard on the exterior, but I don't believe it." I shook my head. "You're not so hard, are you?"

"I like it hard."

"Who are you, Jaxon Cade?"

"That's not any—" He started, but I interrupted him.

"I know it's not my business. I'm no one, yada yada yada." I smiled at him and then gasped as he pinched my nipple hard. "But I want to get to know you better. You're an enigma. You told me things you didn't have to. We're friends."

"With benefits." He grinned.

"You could say that." I moved closer to him. "You don't make me feel bad, you know."

"Bad about what?"

"Your comments. I feel like you're deliberately trying to goad or disparage me, but you're not. I like it when you touch me. I'm attracted to you. My body wants you. My brain is intrigued by you. I like this."

I grabbed his hand and pushed it down. I held my breath as I realized what I was doing. I saw Jaxon's eyes widen as I pushed his hand between my legs and against my wet pussy.

"Yes, I'm already wet." I gasped as I felt his fingers moving of their own volition against me. "I'm doing this because I want to."

"Because you want to be with me?" His words were light, and I moaned as he rubbed me urgently.

I was about to nod when I saw the door to my bedroom open slightly and a face peek in.

"Hunter!" I gasped out, and the door closed quickly.

I looked to see if Jaxon had witnessed Hunter poking his head through the door as well, but he looked at me with a disgusted expression and dropped his hand. It was then that I realized that he thought I'd been correcting him. He thought I was doing all of this with him because I wanted to be with Hunter.

I lay back and stared at the ceiling as my heart thudded. If I were smart, I'd be thinking about Hunter, but I knew that, while I still thought Hunter was cute, he hadn't really been on my mind since I'd met Jaxon. There was something about Jaxon that captivated me. He was so completely unlike all of the other men I'd ever thought about or daydreamed about, but he was also better than all of my daydreams combined. He took my body on highs I hadn't even known existed.

However, I knew I wasn't going to tell him that. There was still a part of me that was unsure if I could trust him. Yes, he'd told me about his father's wanting revenge on Brandon, but I wasn't sure if that was the whole story. Something was still extremely fishy, and I was not leaving until I had it all figured out.

CHAPTER SEVEN

Jaxon

I hadn't thought hearing Nancy say Hunter's name would have affected me as much as it had. My blood was boiling hot. I couldn't believe that she was still muttering his name. I was positive that she was doing it to rile me up and make me jealous. Little did she know that I didn't get jealous. I would never be jealous of her wanting that wannabe man. He was nothing. I could crush him with my bare hands. The fact that she thought he was cute told me a lot about her state of mind.

What smart woman would ever think he was cute? Would ever be in a bed with me and calling out his name? I felt my face heating up as I stared at her naked body next to mine. She was too damn sexy for her own good. My cock was hard with desire and about to burst. I wanted to take her so badly. I could almost feel how good it would be inside of her. Her pussy would be wet and tight as I entered her hard and fast. Her lips would part slightly and she would cry out in pleasure as I gave her orgasm after orgasm. She'd never think of Hunter's name again. All she'd be able to say is, "Jaxon, please. Jaxon, please."

I ran my fingers across her stomach, and she rolled over on top of me. I was surprised at her movements and still angry at her for saying his name.

"You have a thing for my lap, don't you?"

"Your lap has a thing for me," she whispered down against my lips as her breasts rubbed against my chest.

"Oh that's not a thing." I grabbed her hips, placed her pussy directly on my bulge, and moved her back and forth so that she was straddling me and rubbing her clit against my hardness. "That's a pleasure maker," I growled as she continued moving her lips back and forth. I closed my eyes and then pushed her off of me. She wasn't allowed to come again until I was positive that she had thoughts only for me. "I'm leaving." I jumped off of the bed.

"Jaxon." She groaned as she lay back on the bed and looked up at me.

"I'll see you later, Nancy." I walked out of the room and didn't look back. I had a feeling that sex was going to be the undoing of Nancy, but what scared me most was that she was going to be the undoing of me.

CHAPTER EIGHT

Nancy

My dreams were filled with Jaxon. Jaxon smiling. Jaxon looking angry. Jaxon touching me. Me on top of Jaxon. I woke up feeling horny and tired. My eyes felt like they were full of sand, and I just felt miserable and confused. I knew that I was in over my head. I knew that I should go home.

The thought of being here and being sexual with a man whose father was trying to take my father down seemed stupid. I wasn't sure what I was accomplishing by letting Jaxon touch me and teach me. I knew if I was honest with myself that I liked it. I liked him more than I wanted to admit and I wanted to experience more of him. I wanted to break his shell and understand him better. I groaned as I realized that I was the epitome of every other girl who met a man who had issues. I wanted to be the one to break through and figure him out. And it was all based on physical chemistry.

I'd been attracted to him since the train. I wanted him. My body wanted him. I didn't even care that I was a virgin. I didn't even care about Hunter. When I was with Jaxon, I felt like I was soaring through the air at a million miles per hour and I never knew if I was going to crash and burn or land on my feet. It was an exhilarating, exciting feeling. It made me feel like I was alive more than anything else had ever made me feel. Jaxon made me feel like Nancy and just Nancy.

Talking to him yesterday had made me realize just how much had happened in my life and so quickly. I was part of a family I hadn't even known existed, and while I loved every single one of them, I sometimes felt like I didn't really belong. And I still felt angry towards Brandon. I tried not to, but a part of me hated him for abandoning my mom and me.

I'd grown up and lived my life for eighteen years and I hadn't even known he was my dad. What hurt more was knowing that he knew I was out there all along and he hadn't even tried to get to know me. He hadn't even tried to be in my life. It hurt me to the core. How could he love me if he hadn't wanted to be in my life? Especially knowing what he'd done for Harry. He'd taken Harry from the beginning. As much as I loved my brother, I was slightly jealous. He was the golden child, born of love. I was the one he'd never wanted.

Sometimes I felt like I didn't fit in with their perfect family. I was the odd one out. A part of me felt that, by staying, I was proving myself and my loyalty and winning their hearts and trust. I also felt like Jaxon was a lost soul as well. Maybe, in fixing him, I could fix myself as well.

I rubbed my fingers across my eyes and sighed. I was a mess. I really didn't know what I was doing or if I was making the right decision by staying.

The ringing phone interrupted my thoughts, and I picked it up gingerly.

"Hello."

"Nancy." It was Meg.

"Hey, what's up?" I exclaimed in an overly happy voice.

"How are you doing?"

"I'm fine."

"You don't sound fine." Her voice lowered. "How is Hunter?"

"He's fine."

"Nancy, what aren't you telling me?"

"There's this guy. Jaxon Cade." I sighed. "He's..."

"Who is Jaxon Cade?" Meg's voice grew louder, and I could hear the worry in her tone.

"Just someone I met. It's fine."

"Nancy, what's going on?" Her tone changed.

"Nothing." I bit my lower lip. I really wanted to tell Meg what I'd found out, but I really didn't want her to get worried or try to handle this for me. I needed to do this by myself.

"Nancy, I think it's time for you to come home."

"I'm fine," I lied and closed my eyes. "I'll be home soon."

"Katie and Brandon have been talking about you a lot. We had dinner with then yesterday. I'm not sure—"

"I gotta go, Meg. I'll speak to you later."

"Nancy, tell me who Jaxon Cade is." Meg's voice was still ringing in my ear as I turned the phone off.

My heart was pounding as I sat up and jumped out of bed. The room seemed to be spinning as I stood upright. I wasn't sure what way was up, and I felt like I was about to faint. I didn't even understand myself and my thoughts. Everything was so confusing to me. I hadn't even realized until that morning that I had resentment for Harry. My heart felt sad at the thought. He loved me more than life itself, yet I was jealous of the relationship he had with our dad.

I sat on the bed and closed my eyes. I could feel tears threatening to fall. I felt sad. And I felt excited. Jaxon excited me. And it was about more than the lust and the sexual attraction. It was about how he made me feel when I was with him. It was about feeling like I was in control for once. This was all me and all him. There was nothing in between us. There was no falsehood. We were both honest about who we were and why we were there. It wasn't pretty, but it was real. As real as the feelings he brought out in me when he touched me. I couldn't leave now. Not when so much was at stake. Not only was I saving my father, I was saving myself as well.

***

I was on my way to breakfast when I saw Hunter walking up the stairs. I slowed my pace and stood back as soon as I saw him. I didn't want to talk to him. I was surprised that I was avoiding him already; I hadn't realized that I could be so fickle.

"It's not like you really knew him," I whispered to myself as I watched him reach the top of the stairs and head down the other side of the landing. It was weird to me that I felt nothing when I stared at him.

I laughed softly to myself as I thought of all the nights I'd spent writing in my journal and making up poems about our love. All it had taken was a couple of conversations with Jaxon and I was already over Hunter. Maybe that was because I'd never had anything real with him.

I was about to head back down the stairs when I saw Jaxon's dad coming up the stairs.

"Hunter," he called out, and I watched as Hunter turned around and walked towards Jaxon's dad.

"Hello, Mr. Cade."

"Come. We need to talk." Jaxon's dad looked down the hallway and grabbed his arm.

"I spoke to her." Hunter shrugged. "Everything's going well."

"She likes you still?"

"She was all over me." Hunter grinned. "Though Jaxon was being an ass."

"He doesn't know about our conversation." The older man frowned.

Hunter shrugged. "Makes no difference to me."

"Blood is thicker than water—unless you're after revenge."

I watched as they got closer to me. Jaxon's father's eyes were devoid of emotion as he spoke to Hunter.

"Some people will do anything for love, and some would do anything for money." Hunter nodded his head.

"That is true." The older man paused. "I have one wish, and I don't care who gets the job done. Whatever happens is of no concern to me."

"Whatever?" Hunter paused as a smile crossed his face.

"Whatever." The older man nodded. "I have no patience for weakness. You have to do whatever you have to do. Even if that means there are other casualties."

"Even if it's Jaxon?"

"Even if it's Jaxon." The older man nodded. "Do what you have to do."

I pressed my body back against the door as I watched them. They were so close to me now. If they took a few more steps, they'd see me. I stayed as still as possible and almost burst into tears as I heard Jaxon's father talk again.

"I better go. I hope to hear some good news soon."

"Yes, sir. I'm on it." Hunter's voice sounded eager, and I wondered exactly what they were talking about. Surely it couldn't have been me? Would Hunter really try to hurt me now that he knew who I was?

My breathing stopped for a moment as it hit me. Hunter didn't know who I was. He'd been coached. That was why he had my last name wrong and why he'd said I'd been in his Spanish class. He had no idea who I was. I meant nothing to him.

I could have laughed out loud at myself if the situation hadn't been so tense. I'd been feeling guilty that I wasn't as into Hunter as I'd thought, but he didn't even remember me. I sobered up as I realized that Jaxon's dad was really serious about getting his revenge. I waited a few minutes and then decided to go to Jaxon's room. I needed to speak to him right away.

***

"Hi." I knocked on Jaxon's door and walked in without waiting for a response.

"I've gotten you into a bad habit, haven't I?" He looked up at me from the floor where he was doing crunches.

I tried not to stare at his bare chest too hard. "I'm learning from the best I suppose."

"What if I'd been in here fucking someone?" He jumped up and stared at me.

"What about it?" I shot back, feeling angry and jealous. What was his problem?

"That's not something I want to be interrupted in the middle of." He snarled at me.

"Well, same goes here. What if I'd been in my room fucking Hunter? I wouldn't want you interrupting me either." I hissed back at him, feeling angry and annoyed. I couldn't believe that I had been starting to think he was a good guy.

"You're not going to fuck, Hunter."

"I'll fuck who I want." I turned around, ready to leave.

"Over my dead body." He grabbed my shoulders and turned me towards him. "You're such a fool."

"I'm a fool?" My voice rose and I glared at him. "More like you. You're a fool."

"I should kiss some sense into you." His nostrils flared as he looked down into my eyes.

"You, Tarzan. Me, Jane." I pummeled my fists against his chest in a weak manner. "Take me, you brute. Show me what a man you are. Make me see some sense." I swung my hair around and rolled my eyes. I saw his lips start to twitch at my act, and his eyes softened.

"You're silly."

"I'm just a woman." I fell against him. "I need you to put some sense into me."

"I'm willing to do whatever you ask." He winked at me, grabbed around my waist, and pulled me towards him. "And if that means fucking you senseless right now, I'm happy to oblige."

"You wish." I gasped as I felt his hardness against me. "Are you always this hard?"

"Only when I see you." He grinned and leaned down to kiss me. His lips were soft against mine as I kissed him back passionately. How could I resist this man? "So now tell me why you barged into my room so eagerly."

"I wasn't being eager." I took a deep breath and flushed.

"That's another lesson I'll have to teach you. Never chase the man, Nancy. Let him come to you."

"I'm not chasing you."

"Really?" He ran his fingers across my lips. "It sure looks that way to me."

"You're such an asshole. I swear, if I didn't want to protect my family, I'd slap you."

"You can slap me." He grinned. "I like a bit of rough."

"You would." I rolled my eyes.

"In fact, I'd like to try a bit of rough with you." He studied my face as he spoke. "If you're willing, of course."

"What do you mean? A bit of rough?" I frowned.

"You'll see." He smacked my ass lightly.

"You're going to spank me?"

"If you're a bad girl."

"Jaxon." I pulled away from him. "We need to talk." I took a deep breath and tried to ignore the urge to run my fingers down his chest. My brain was starting to feel hazy again.

"About?" He cocked his head to the side.

"I think your dad and Hunter are planning something."

"I see." He stared back at me, unblinking.

"That's it? Aren't you going to ask what?"

"Don't worry about it." He shook his head and took a step towards me. "We have more important things to discuss."

"Jaxon, I'm worried."

"Don't be." He grabbed my hands.

"I need to know the plan." I frowned. "I need to know what we're going to do. I understand that your dad wants you to use me to get to my dad, but what next? When does this end?"

"Let me worry about that, Nancy," he whispered against my lips. "I've got a plan."

"What are we going to do about Hunter?" I bit my lower lip.

"I've got a plan for him too." His eyes darkened. "Just don't get any ideas around him."

"If he can't resist me, then what can I say?" I shot back at him, trying to get a rise out of him.

I knew I'd succeeded when he took a step away from me and his face turned to a grimace. A surge of electricity jolted through me as I realized that bringing up Hunter was a sure way to get a reaction from Jaxon.

"I already told you not to play with fire, Nancy." His eyes were cold. "It's not just you who's going to get burned."

***

"I want you to wear this tonight." He walked to the side of his room, picked up a plastic bag, and handed it to me.

I took it from him slowly, still feeling jolted by his words. "What is it?" I asked curiously, picturing some see-through top or negligee.

"You'll see."

I opened the bag and peered in. Whatever he had given me was black. However, it was the other item in the bag that made my heart race. "Is this a whip?" I pulled it out eagerly, examining it carefully.

"Yes."

"What for?"

"You'll see." He smiled, and I watched his eyes light up in mischief. "Tonight is going to be a very educational evening."

"You're determined to push all of my boundaries, aren't you?"

"I just want to be the best teacher that I can be."

"I don't want to get hurt." I looked into his eyes. "I don't want either one of us to get hurt."

"Why do you care about me, Nancy?" He frowned. "You should be thinking about self-preservation, not about me."

"Caring about what happens to you doesn't mean I don't care about myself." I shook my head. "What do you think I should do? Just worry about myself?"

"Where has caring about others gotten you?" He raised an eyebrow at me. "Used."

"Are you using me?" I looked at the plastic bag in my hand. "Don't bother answering that."

"I'm not made for love or relationships, but I'm not a user, Nancy. I hope you know me well enough by now to know that."

"What do I know?" I shrugged. "You don't trust any of my other thoughts or concerns."

"When I was fifteen, I met a girl." His eyes bored into mine. "She was gorgeous. Big, bright-blue eyes, long blond hair, a smile that tugged at my heartstrings."

"And?" I looked down, suddenly overcome with jealousy.

"We became friends. I thought she was going to become my girlfriend." He laughed bitterly. "I went out and bought her a necklace. 24-karat gold." His face was full of derision. "I gave it to her. She was so happy. I thought to myself, 'This is it. This is the beginning of something beautiful.'"

"What happened?"

"I saw her laughing with her friends the next day, showing off my necklace. She said she was going to try for a watch next." His face twisted.

"I'm sorry." I stepped forward. "You must have been heartbroken."

"I was hurt. I went to my father and told him what happened." His eyes were bright with remembered emotions.

"What did he say?"

"He told me to take the bitch down." His mouth twisted. "So I met her the next day and I pretended that I knew nothing. She gave me that sweet smile and I was nearly caught by her web of lies again."

"What happened?" My breath caught as I waited for his answer.

"I took her out to dinner." He shrugged. "I left a $25,000 Rolex on the table next to her. Then I got up and called the police."

"The police?" I frowned.

"The Rolex was stolen." He smiled. "My dad gave it to me."

"Oh my God. What happened?"

"She got arrested." He laughed. "She wasn't charged, but it gave her a fright. She knew not to mess with me after that day."

"And ever since then, you've been against women and relationships?"

"All women want is stuff. They want love. Or they want sex. They want gifts or someone to listen to them. But it's never enough. They just want, want, want. With no real care as to the man they are with. We're expendable."

"Men aren't expendable. And it does matter who you are."

"Does it matter to you, Nancy?" He turned to me. "You came for Hunter. You espouse concern and like for him, yet here you are with me. What do you want from me?"

"I don't want anything from you," I shot back at him hurt. "I'm not a user."

"We don't really know what either of us is, do we?"

"I'm sorry that girl hurt you so much, Jaxon, but she was one girl, and if I'm honest, that story isn't even all that bad. I know plenty of guys who have gone through much worse, yet they are still giving love a chance."

"I don't give two shits about love."

"Point taken."

"Don't tell me that you hope to have the white picket fence and all that jazz?" His eyes narrowed as he looked at me.

"I hope to meet the man of my dreams, yes. I hope to get married. I hope to have kids. I hope to fall in love slowly and deliciously." I could feel my heart breaking as I spoke. I had such high hopes, such dreams when it came to love, but a part of me didn't believe, not really and truly, that any of it would come true.

"Young and foolish."

"And you're old and wise?" I asked him softly.

"Do you truly believe in love, Nancy?" He cocked his head to the side. "Do you truly believe that you have a soul mate out there whose soul purpose is to make you happy?"

"I don't know," I answered honestly, not really knowing how to respond. "My heart wants to believe. My soul wants to believe. I want to believe with every fiber of my being, but I just don't know."

"One thing we do know is that we have this." He pointed at the space between us. "We have magnetism. We have attraction. We have this."

"It's sex." I shrugged. "Let's not call it something it isn't."

"I want to take you on a journey, Nancy. A journey that has no boundaries. A journey that's exciting and death defying. A journey you've never experienced before." He sighed. "We came into this situation for two different reasons, yet I think we can move forward in a way that benefits us both."

"My first concern is to keeping my family safe."

"Nothing will happen to them. You have my word."

CHAPTER NINE

Jaxon

The latex bodysuit fit her perfectly. She stood there looking confident, whip in hand, ready to get started. I smiled to myself at her fake poise. She might look the part, but she had absolutely no idea what I had in store for her. The night was just beginning, and I was ready to show her just how much pleasure one could get from power.

I spoke up as I approached her. "I see you've put on the outfit."

She turned towards me with widened eyes, her fingers gripping the whip tightly. "You want me to whip you?" She smiled at me wickedly as she showed off the whip.

"No." I smiled to myself. She was already getting into the role.

"Then what?" she mumbled, looking at me with pouty lips. The red lipstick was stark on her pale face. It made her look older, more sophisticated, more sexual and in charge. I shifted as I realized that I was already turned on.

"What do you think?" I walked closer to her and grabbed the whip.

"You're not going to hit me." Her eyes widened, and I could see her lips trembling.

"Are you scared it's going to hurt?"

"What do you think?" She rolled her eyes and tried to pull the whip back and out of my palms.

"I'm not going to whip you." I smiled and let go of the whip.

"Oh." She looked up at me and I saw a quick flash of disappointment in her eyes. The emotion surprised me as I'd been expecting to see relief and only relief.

"We're going to use ropes."

"Ropes?" She looked confused. "What for?"

"Fun." I smiled.

"So you're not going to tell me?"

"We're not using ropes right now."

"Oh." She sounded surprised. "What are we doing right now?"

"Tonight, we're going out."

"Out?" She looked disappointed.

"A little birdie told me you wanted to go to a club." I took a step towards her and watched the pulse in her neck throbbing.

"Club?" She shook her head.

"Yes, club. Music, people, dancing."

"First of all, you dance?" She smiled and then paused. "And I'm going dressed like this?"

"I'm a man of many surprises, Nancy." I kissed her neck, no longer able to stop from touching her. The latex felt edgy and sexy beneath my fingers as I ran my fingertips across her breasts. "I want to pull this suit off of you," I growled into her ear as my hand caressed her ass.

"Try it and maybe you'll be the one feeling the whip," she murmured.

I pulled back and saw a glint in her eyes. She had a smirk on her face, and I started to wonder if the student was about to overtake the teacher.

"Maybe tonight, I'll let you." I grinned at her and pressed my lips against hers.

I felt a stirring in the pit of my stomach that I tried to ignore. Everything was going so perfectly, and I was starting to feel something I'd never felt before. I was starting to feel attached. Part of me worried that the plan was going to backfire. The other part of me was worried that everything was going to go perfectly. I wasn't sure what I wanted to happen anymore. I'd never anticipated Nancy's being someone who would change the rules. I'd never anticipated that I'd want the rules changed.

CHAPTER TEN

Nancy

I walked with Amber and Shannon into the club. Jaxon was with Hunter and Keenan, and they were a few yards ahead of us. Staring at Jaxon next to Hunter, I wondered how I had ever been attracted to Hunter. He was a boy when compared to Jaxon. I shivered as I stared at Jaxon's back, so strong and muscular.

"What sort of club is this?" Amber's eyes were full of excitement as she looked around the dark club.

"I have no idea." My eyes looked around the dark room. There were couples dancing, couples making out, and I was pretty sure that there were a few couples having sex. "No club I've been to before I'm sure."

"It's a sex club," Shannon whispered and gave me a weak smile. "Hunter told me before we came."

"Oh?" I looked at her in surprise.

For some reason, I always seemed to forget that she was paired with Hunter. I wondered if I should warn her that there was a possibility that he was bad news, but I knew that there was a possibility that it would look like I had sour grapes if I said anything.

"He asked me if I wanted to wear something sexier." Shannon looked embarrassed, and I tried to ignore the fact that she was wearing a pair of baggy jeans and a plaid shirt.

"You look fine." I smiled at her.

"She looks like a fucking redneck." Amber started laughing. "Who wears a plaid shirt to the club? A wannabe cowgirl. Shit, even cowgirls know how to sex it up."

"Amber, that's not cool." I shook my head and frowned. She was really starting to get on my nerves.

"I'm just saying it like it is." Amber gave me a piercing look. "Let's be real. Even you've slutted it up tonight."

"Excuse me?" I stared at her in her tiny crop top and miniskirt. Was she really calling me a slut?

"Girl, you are wearing a latex catsuit with no underwear. Or did you think we couldn't tell you didn't have a panty line?" Amber stared at my ass. "And your nipples are popping out. I'd say that you and Mr. Jaxon seem to be getting on real well, real fast."

"Whatever." I rolled my eyes and looked away from her.

"So tell me." She took a step closer to me.

"Tell you what?"

"How big is his cock?" She grinned.

"Amber!" Shannon grabbed her arm. "Come on. That's enough."

"Why are both of you such prudes?" Amber started dancing to the music as two hot bouncers walked past us. "We go to a sex school, yet you both act like Virgin Marys."

"We don't go to a sex school." I bit my lower lip as I realized that she was correct. At the end of the day, we were at a sex school.

I stared at Amber and Shannon for a few seconds and started laughing. They both looked at me like I was crazy, but I couldn't stop laughing.

"What's so funny?" Jaxon walked back towards me and gave me a questioning look.

"You don't want to know?" I gasped as I continued laughing.

"Try me." He smiled at me and then looked me up and down. "Damn, you look sexy in that bodysuit."

"I know. You've told me about five times." I grinned, feeling sexy and confident.

"Every man in here wants you."

"Oh really?" I looked around the room. "I guess I should decide who I want to be with."

"You're not going to be with anyone but me." He growled and pulled me towards him. "Now tell me. What's so funny?"

I shook my head. "You don't want to know."

"Tell me." He kissed me lightly and sucked on my lower lip.

"I was just thinking. You said the Lovers' Academy is really a front for training high-class escorts, right?"

"Uh huh." He nodded, his eyes staring into mine curiously.

"I don't get how Amber and Shannon fit in." I giggled. "I can't see them being high-class escorts. No offense or anything, but they are the last two I'd think of as being girls of the night to the rich and famous."

"Yeah." He nodded thoughtfully. "That's a good point. I suppose my father has his reasons."

"I mean, Amber's mouth would get her into trouble." I shook my head and giggled.

His hands slid to my ass as he whispered in my ear, "What's so funny?"

"I was just picturing Amber asking some rich guy how big his dick was."

He laughed as squeezed my ass. "Why?"

"Because she's asked me several times how big you are."

"Oh yeah?" He pulled back and smiled down at me. "She has?"

"Yes." I frowned at the look on his face. "Don't tell me you think that's a compliment."

"If she's curious, I should tell her, no?"

"No." I pulled away from him annoyed.

"Shall we go and dance?" He grabbed my hands, and I followed him silently.

I was pissed that he'd even consider telling Amber anything. Would he let her touch it too if she asked? I could feel my face going red as I grew angrier and angrier.

"Amber, want to come dance with us?" he called out to her as we walked past the group, and I pulled away from him silently.

We all crowded onto the dance floor, and I watched as Amber and her teacher, Keenan, bumped and grinded. His hands were under her top, squeezing her breasts, and I could see her thrusting her ass into him.

"She's a sexy dancer," Jaxon whispered into my ear as we stood there.

"Glad you think so," I snapped at him and turned away from him.

We stood there standing next to each other, dancing awkwardly. I wasn't sure what I'd expected, but it hadn't been me standing here with Jaxon while he watched Amber gyrating.

Hunter walked over to me with a dopey grin and a blank look in his eyes. "Want to dance, Nancy?"

I wasn't really interested in dancing with him, but I wanted Jaxon to be jealous. I wanted his attention to be on me and not on Amber. Why the fuck would he bring me to a sex club wearing a catsuit that clung to my body if he wasn't even going to try anything?

"Sure." I walked towards Hunter and knew immediately that Jaxon's eyes were now on me.

I kept my gaze averted from him as I put my hands into the air and started moving to the music. There was a power in the air, and I could feel the hairs on the back of my neck rising as I danced in beat to the music, shimmying my hips to the ground and up again. Hunter grabbed me around the waist, and I could feel his hands around my stomach as he danced with the beat to the music. I closed my eyes and started swinging my hips in a more pronounced fashion as I shook my head and let my hair fall across my face.

"You're so sexy, Nancy," Hunter whispered into my ear. "You were pretty back in school, but right now, you're just plain sexy. You turn me on so much."

He brought me back against him, and I felt something pressed against my ass. I was about to pull forward when I saw

Jaxon staring at me with manic eyes, looking pissed. I smiled at him sweetly and then started moving even more rhythmically, pretending I was a stripper and Hunter was my pole.

"Oh yeah, baby," Hunter growled into my ear.

It was then that I felt his hands move up from my waist to my breasts. I froze in shock as I felt his hands squeezing my breasts.

"Get your hands off of her."

Before I knew it, Jaxon was next to us, and he was pulling me away from Hunter. His fists were clenched, and I watched as he punched Hunter.

"Jaxon, stop!" I grabbed his shoulders and pulled him back.

"Whoa, dude." Hunter looked dazed as he rubbed his jaw.

"Don't fucking touch her." Jaxon leaned towards him. "Or I'll make you forget the day you were born."

"It's not my fault she wants me." Hunter shrugged and looked at me. "She's always wanted me. Shit, she was practically begging for me to take her."

"You're playing with fire, Hunter." Jaxon grabbed his shirt. "I'm telling you that you're messing with the wrong guy."

"You're not the only one who can make threats, Jaxon." Hunter's face changed and he leaned forward. "Only, I usually follow through with my threats." Hunter ran his hands through his hair. "You're not going to be able to come to her rescue every single time." He laughed and then looked at me. "Remember why you came here, Nancy. Don't let Jaxon fool you. I can protect you. Just come to me when you figure it out." With that, he turned away and I was left with Jaxon, who was looking very, very angry.

"What did you just do?" I looked at Jaxon in anger. "Why would you hit him?"

"He touched you." His eyes were wide and his expression was grim.

"That was for me to deal with. Not you."

"Did you want him to touch you?" He grabbed my wrists. "Do you want to be with him?"

"Jaxon." I squirmed and tried to pull my wrists away. "You're hurting me."

"Did you want him to touch you?" he asked me again. This time, his voice was softer.

"No," I said finally, my eyes staring into his. "I'm not interested in being touched by him."

"Why did you do it then?"

"You were staring at Amber."

"Jealousy is the beginning of the end." He pursed his lips.

"You were jealous too."

"There was nothing to be jealous of." He shook his head as if denying the emotion.

"Fine. Can we just leave?" I sighed. "I'm not having fun."

He shook his head. "The night hasn't even started."

"What do you mean?"

"I'm about to teach you about punishment."

"Punishment?" I shivered as he stared at me with a slight smile.

"It's your lesson for the night." He reached over and touched my face lightly.

"You're going to use the whip?" My eyes widened.

"No." He shook his head and bit down on my neck. "Tonight, we're going to use the ropes."

CHAPTER ELEVEN

Jaxon

I was so angry at Nancy as I led her to the private room. I couldn't believe she'd danced so recklessly with that piece of scum. I'd thought I was going to rip his head off when I saw him touching her and her smiling. I wanted to wipe the smile off her face. It didn't make me feel better to know that she'd been dancing with him to make me jealous. I didn't even think about the fact that I'd been trying to make her jealous by pretending to be interested in the bimbo, Amber.

I wasn't sure where my father had gotten Amber and Shannon from, but I wasn't surprised that Nancy had questioned their validity at being at the Lovers' Academy. I was just lucky that she hadn't asked too many more questions about their acceptance to the academy. She was already too close to the truth.

"Take the catsuit off," I commanded as we walked into the room.

"What?" She frowned.

"Take it off." I didn't smile as I locked the door.

"What are you going to do?"

"You'll have to wait and see."

"I see." She nibbled her lower lip and slowly started pulling the catsuit off.

I stared at her naked body in admiration and lust. I wanted her so badly. I was surprised that I hadn't already had her. I'd never waited this long before. Normally, I took what I wanted and never looked back, but it was different with her. I didn't want it to just be about the sex. I didn't want her to feel used. I wanted her to feel special.

I frowned at the thought. I was getting soft. I'd never cared about anyone else thinking it was going to be special. But it was different with her. I almost groaned as I thought about the story I'd made up about being fifteen and getting my heart broken. She'd seen it for what it was and called me out. I loved that about her. Though I didn't think she wanted to know the truth. That I'd been fifteen and fucking my friend's older sister when her parents had caught us and demanded my father put a stop to my going over to their house.

He'd put a stop to it all right. I'd stopped going there, but several older and more thuggish men had shown up in my place.

They'd left town within a few months, and my father had laughed. No one told a Cade what to do. Never.

"What now?" Nancy's voice interrupted my thoughts.

I stared at her again. There was something so vulnerable in her gaze. Something that made me pause. Something that made me think I had a heart buried somewhere deep inside.

"Come towards me." I bent down, opened a chest to the right of the door, and pulled out a coil of rope.

"What are you going to do?" she asked softly.

"Shhh." I placed a finger against her lips and started wrapping the rope around her body. She trembled slightly as I quickly worked it around her. "It's not going to hurt." I stopped and stared at the rope tied around her body. "Trust me."

"I don't know about this." She nibbled on her lower lip.

"I'm going to tie your wrists and your ankles next."

"And?"

"Then I'm going to use the pinwheel."

"The pinwheel?" She frowned at me, her brown eyes wide in anticipation.

"You'll see." I smiled as I stared into her eyes.

I was going to enjoy taking over every fiber of her body. Soon, all she would be able to think about was me and what I was doing to her. Soon, she'd be begging me for release from the sweet, sharp pain that was going to drive both of us crazy.

"I'm scared," she whispered.

"Don't be scared." I looked into her eyes and took a deep breath. "It's going to be pleasurable."

"I don't know." She looked panicked as I led her to the bed.

"Lie down," I commanded. "Spread your arms and your legs wide open."

She stared at me in thought for a second and then spread her legs open wide. I gasped as I looked at her beautiful body waiting for me, trusting me. I felt a dull ache shifting in me as I stared at her. She was too beautiful, too trusting. She was already in too deep, and she was taking me under with her with every step that went by.

I tied her wrists and ankles to the four bedpost corners and stepped back. I was ready to get started.

"Are you ready?" I whispered as I walked to the chest and pulled out the pinwheel.

She nodded, and I saw her eyes open as she stared at the instrument in my hands. The handle was about six inches long and the pins all around the circle looked more sharp than dull.

"Use me like I'm a parachute. I'll open if you fall." I leaned forward and ran a finger down her leg before replacing my finger with the pinwheel.

"I don't want to fall," she whispered as she squirmed on the bed.

"I don't want to open," I whispered back.

I didn't tell her that I was scared that I'd be a faulty parachute. I didn't tell her that there was a possibility that we were both going to crash and fall, because nothing could save us then.

CHAPTER TWELVE

Nancy

The pinwheel that Jaxon was running across my body had a weird feeling. Just as I thought it was going to become too painful, a jolt of pleasure would run through my body. It was sharp and tingly all at the same time. Every nerve in my body was on edge. Every piece of my skin wanted to be touched. My arms were starting to ache, and I was starting to feel weak from the pleasure resounding through my body.

Jaxon's face looked determined and handsome as he teased me. I caught him staring at me every few seconds to see how I felt. I could see the look of concern in his eyes. It was equal to the look of desire and excitement. He was getting off on teasing me. He was enjoying that I was enjoying it.

"Tell me if it hurts and I'll stop," he told me for the fourth time. "I don't want it to hurt."

"It doesn't hurt," I whispered.

"I'm not pressing it in too hard. I don't want it to hurt."

"I thought you wanted to hurt me. Isn't that why you call it punishment?" I groaned as he ran it lightly across my clit. "Oh."

"No." He smiled at me as he let his pinky finger rub me gently. "The punishment comes later."

"What's the punishment?" I groaned. What could be more tantalizing than this?

"The punishment comes from need." He grinned, and I watched as he took his shirt off and then his pants.

He stood in front of me in just his boxer shorts, and I stared at the bulge in his pants with wide eyes. His fingers reached his boxer shorts, and I watched him pull them down slowly until he was standing in front of me naked.

"What are you going to do?" I whispered eagerly. I wanted to reach out and touch him, but my hands were tied tight.

"What do you want me to do?" He crawled onto the bed next to me.

"Touch me," I whispered.

"How do you want me to touch you?" He leaned down, took my nipple between his teeth, and sucked. "Like this?" he muttered as he switched to my other nipple.

I squirmed on the bed underneath him. His lips felt delicious on my skin. "Yes," I groaned and then moaned as he pulled away.

"Or would you rather I touch you like this?" His fingers ran down my stomach to my pussy and he gently ran his fingers over my clit. I felt myself growing wet as he played with me. "Or would you rather have my cock instead of my fingers?" He shifted his body on top of me, and I felt his cock between my legs, rubbing roughly against my clit.

"Oh, yes," I groaned as he backed away. "Please don't stop!" I cried as he pulled away from me, every fiber of my being wanting him to continue.

"Or would you rather have my mouth?" He grinned at me before he buried his face in my pussy.

I felt his tongue licking up my juices before it slowly entered me. My hands clenched, and I closed my eyes as I felt the tip of his tongue inside me.

"More please," I whispered as his tongue left me. "Please."

"Maybe it's time for you to please me." He moved up the bed. "I'm going to turn around and I want you to take me in your mouth."

"Okay." I nodded eagerly, wanting to pleasure him as much as he was pleasuring me.

I felt his cock rubbing against my mouth and I opened it eagerly, taking his hardness in and sucking on it with as much intensity as I could. He moved his hips back and forth as I sucked as if he were fucking my mouth, and I groaned as I realized how much I was enjoying it. He tasted salty and hard, and I knew in that moment that nothing had ever tasted so good before in my life. I knew he was enjoying what I was doing because I heard him groaning and felt his body stilling as I sucked on him.

"What are you doing?" I cried as he pulled out of my mouth and turned around.

He leaned down and kissed me softly before grinning. "This is your punishment." He ran his fingers over my trembling lips. "You shall neither come nor make me come tonight."

"What?" I groaned as I tried to lean up. "Please."

"Don't try and make me jealous again." His eyes darkened. "I won't be so gentle next time."

"That's it?" I moaned as he untied my wrists. I reached out and touched his chest, and he laughed.

"That's it, Nancy. You're not ready for the next step yet." He stared at my body one last time and sighed. "Now it's time for us to go home."

CHAPTER THIRTEEN

Jaxon

I knew that I was going to have to whack off as soon as I got to my room. My cock was rock hard, and it had taken everything in me to walk away from Nancy without fucking her. Every part of her body was sweet as candy, and I knew that, when I finally took her, it was going to be the best sex I'd ever had.

I opened the door to my bedroom, my mind preoccupied with the image of Nancy on the bed spread-eagle. I groaned as I thought about her, so sweet and innocent and trusting. I was so preoccupied with thoughts of her that I didn't even notice the two men in the room until it was too late.

"Sit down," a voice commanded, and I froze.

I looked up and sighed as I saw who it was. "What are you doing here?" I asked casually and calmly, as if I didn't know exactly why they were here.

"You dare to fuck with my daughter?" Brandon's eyes were dark and his face was murderous.

"I don't know what you're talking about." I shrugged.

"You don't?" He stood up, and it was then that I saw the gun in his hands.

"What's going on, Brandon?"

"I wouldn't play dumb right now, Jaxon." Greyson's voice was harsh. "I wouldn't want Brandon to do something you'd both regret."

"What do you guys want?" I stared at Brandon for a few seconds, and I could feel the blood draining from my face as my heart sank.

This was the end. There was no coming back from this for me. I closed my eyes and sighed. I felt sad—not because my life was flashing before my eyes, but because I hadn't gotten to tell Nancy everything I'd wanted to say. And I hadn't been able to enjoy the night of my life with her.

I opened my eyes and looked at her father with a resigned look on my face. I also felt shocked inside as I realized that I was more worried that I'd never get to talk to her again as opposed to never getting to sleep with her. I knew that I cared for her more than that. Sex was the base of my attraction to her, but it wasn't the only reason I felt drawn to her.

CHAPTER FOURTEEN

Nancy

"So I thought you'd like to know." Shannon gave me a small, shy smile.

"Thanks." I smiled back at her gratefully. "I'm not sure what to think."

"I guess he really likes you." She shrugged. "I heard Amber talking to Keenan and he said that Jaxon has never had anything to do with the academy before you got here."

"I don't understand why he would want to teach me though."

"He must like you." She grinned and leaned forward. "I mean, I saw the way he was looking at you last night. He has the hots for you."

"That's his job though." I sighed and looked down.

I wanted to believe that Jaxon liked me as more than a random stranger, and I did in a way. He wouldn't have told me about his dad and his plans for revenge if he didn't like me at all, but was it enough? Was I special? Was I more than a quick dalliance? That, I didn't know.

"Yeah, but he..." Shannon stopped. "I guess you'll find out soon."

"Find out what?" I frowned, wanting her to continue.

"I shouldn't say." She shook her head. "It's not my place to say."

"Tell me."

"Well, apparently, he never waits for sex." Her eyes were wide as she spoke in hushed tones. "Apparently, that's a sign that he likes you more than he's letting on."

"I see." I nodded, but my insides were burning up with hope.

It had been something I'd been thinking about all night. Why hadn't he had sex with me yet? I had felt and seen how much he'd wanted me. His penis had been rock hard as he had rubbed it against me and when I'd taken him in my mouth. I was pretty sure that he'd been close to coming. I knew that he'd been punishing himself as much as he'd been punishing me when he'd untied me and we'd left. I knew that he wanted me. I knew that it had to have been hard for him to walk away without getting something. If he was a complete and utter jerk, he would have come in my mouth. He had denied himself as well as me. That had to mean something, didn't it?

"Should we go downstairs?"

"Yeah, let's do that." I nodded, eager to go downstairs and see Jaxon.

I was excited to find out what my lesson was for the day. I wanted to see him and kiss him. I wanted to tell him that I was ready for us to go to the next step. As Shannon and I left the room, I realized for the first time since I'd been at the academy that I was really happy. Yes, there was still danger, and yes, I still didn't know what was going to happen, but I had Jaxon. And I knew that, with Jaxon on my side, I could get through anything.

***

They say that time never stands still when you're really happy. It always goes in fast forward. But when things start to go bad, time stands still. It's like the world pauses so that you can experience every last emotion, every last drop of pain. I knew that something had happened as soon as I walked down the stairs and into the foyer with Shannon. It was too quiet, and I shivered as soon as we walked towards the dining hall even though the temperature was warm.

"Nancy, there you are." Amber ran out to greet me, her eyes wild and her usual grin gone.

"Yes, I'm here. Did you need me?" I tried not to sound annoyed, but she was the last person I wanted to see.

"No, not me." She bit her lower lip and paused before she continued. "The police would like to talk to you."

"The police?" I frowned, my heartbeat slowing down.

"He's dead, Nancy." Her voice rose as she grabbed my shoulders.

"What?" I froze, staring at her in disbelief. "Who? How? What?" My hands rose to my forehead.

"He was murdered." The blood ran from her face. "And they think it's because of you."

"Me?" My jaw dropped, but all I could think was, *Who is the he?*

"He had a piece of paper in his hand. It had your name on it."

"What?"

"He's dead because of you, Nancy." Her eyes glittered. "You got him killed."

"Who?" I whispered, my mind going to Jaxon and Hunter. Which one of them had I gotten killed?

I closed my eyes and took a deep breath as my heart broke. I knew that there was one person I wanted alive more than the other, but if he was still alive, it likely meant that he was also the killer. And I wasn't sure how I felt about that, no matter the reason.

AUTHOR'S NOTE

The final book in the series The Love Trials, The Love Trials Part III is available.

Please join my mailing list to be notified of my upcoming releases and teasers: http://jscooperauthor.com/mail-list.

Thank you for reading and purchasing this book. I love to hear from readers so feel free to send me an email at jscooperauthor@gmail.com at any time.

You can also join me on my Facebook page: https://www.facebook.com/J.S.Cooperauthor.

LIST OF AVAILABLE J. S. COOPER BOOKS

You can see a list of all my books on my website: https://www.facebook.com/J.S.Cooperauthor.

The Forever Love Boxed Set (Books 1-3)

Crazy Beautiful Love

The Ex Games

The Private Club

After The Ex Games

Everlasting Sin

Scarred

Healed

The Last Boyfriend

The Last Husband

Before Lucky

The Other Side of Love

Zane & Lucky's First Christmas

LIST OF BOOKS AVAILABLE
FOR PREORDER

ILLUSION

The day started like every other day...

Bianca London finds herself kidnapped and locked up in a van with a strange man. Ten hours later, they're dumped on a deserted island. Bianca has no idea what's going on and her attraction to this stranger is the only thing keeping her fear at bay.

Jakob Bradley wants only to figure out why they've been left on the island and how they can get off. But as the days go by, he can't ignore his growing fascination with Bianca.

In order to survive, Bianca and Jakob must figure out how they're connected, but as they grow closer, secrets are revealed that may destroy everything they thought they knew about each other.

TAMING MY PRINCE CHARMING

When Lola met Xavier, Prince of Romerius, she was immediately attracted to his dark, handsome good looks and sparkling green eyes. She spent a whirlwind weekend with him and almost fell for his charm, until he humiliated her and she fled.

Lola wasn't prepared to find out that Xavier was her new professor and her new boss. She also wasn't prepared for the sparks that flew every time they were together. When Xavier takes her on a work trip, she is shocked when they are mobbed by the paparazzi and agrees to go to Romerius with Xavier to pretend she is his fiancé.

Only Lola had no idea that Xavier had a master plan from the moment he met her. He wanted a week to make her his, so that he could get her out of his system. Only Xavier had no idea that fate had another plan for him.

GUARDING HIS HEART

Leonardo Maxwell was shocked when his best friend, Zane Beaumont fell in love and got married. While he is happy for his friend, he knows that he definitely doesn't want to go the love and marriage route. He knows that there is nothing that can come from either of the two.

When his father calls him and tells him that it's time for him to take over the family business, he does so reluctantly. He's never liked the attention he gets as a billionaire's son, but he knows it's his duty.

Leo is not prepared for the animosity that he gets from his new assistant, Hannah on his first day of work. He has no idea why she hates him, but he's glad for it. He doesn't have time to waste staring at her beautiful long legs or her pink luscious lips. As far as he's concerned they can have a strictly professional relationship. However, that all changes when they go on their first work trip together.

IF ONLY ONCE (THE MARTELLI BROTHERS)

It's the quiet ones that can surprise you

Vincent Martelli grew up as the quiet one in his family. While his brothers got into trouble, he tried to take the studious route, even though he always found himself caught up in their mess.

When Vincent is paired up with a no-nonsense girl in one of his classes, he is frustrated and annoyed. Katia is everything he doesn't want in a woman and yet, he can't seem to get her out of his mind.

Then Katia shows up at his house with his brother's girlfriend, Maddie and he finds himself offering her his bed, when her car breaks down. When Katia accepts he is shocked, but he vows to himself that he won't let down his walls. As far as he is concerned there is no way that he could date someone like her. Only life never does seem to go as planned, does it?

REDEMPTION

One fight can change everything

Hudson Blake has two weeks to get his best friend Luke ready for the fight of his life. If Luke wins the championship he will receive one million dollars to help out the family of the woman he loved and lost.

Hudson's girlfriend, Riley doesn't want Hudson or Luke to fight and so she enlists the help of her best friend, Eden. However, Riley didn't count on Eden finding a battered and bruised Luke sexy and charismatic.

Luke has never felt as alive as he does practicing for the championship. He has vowed that he is not going to let anything get in his way. He knows that he is fighting for redemption and love. And he can't afford to lose.

THE ONLY WAY

Jared Martelli is the youngest Martelli brother, but he's also the most handsome and most confident. There is nothing that gets in the way of what he wants and he has no time for love.

Jared blows off college to start his own business and it's his goal to make a million dollars within five years. He's happy working hard and playing the field. That is until he meets Pippa one night at a bar. Pippa is headstrong, beautiful and has absolutely no interest in him. And that's one thing Jared can't accept.

He decides to pursue Pippa with plans of dropping her once she submits to his charms. Only his plans go awry when he realizes that Pippa has plans of her own and they don't include him.

TO YOU, FROM ME

Sometimes the greatest gifts in life come when you least expect them

Zane Beaumont never expected to fall in love with Lucky Morgan. He never expected to have a household full of children. He never knew that his life could be so full of laughter and love.

To You, From Me chronicles Zane and Lucky's relationship from the good times to the bad. It shows why marriage can be the best and worst experience in your life. Experience the gamut of emotions that Zane goes through as he goes through the journey of being a husband and father.

CRAZY BEAUTIFUL CHRISTMAS

Logan, Vincent and Jared Martelli decide to spend Christmas together with the women they love. Only none of their plans are going right. When they find a pregnancy test all three of them start to panic about becoming a father. Only they don't know which one of them is the daddy to be.

Join the Martelli Brothers on their quest for the perfect Christmas holiday. They may have a few more bumps in the road than they planned, but ultimately it will be the season of giving and loving.

ABOUT THE AUTHOR

J. S. Cooper was born in London, England and moved to Florida her last year of high school. After completing law school at the University of Iowa (from the sunshine to cold) she moved to Los Angeles to work for a Literacy non profit as an Americorp Vista. She then moved to New York to study the History of Education at Columbia University and took a job at a workers rights non profit upon graduation.

She enjoys long walks on the beach (or short), hot musicians, dogs, reading (duh) and lots of drama filled TV Shows.

Made in the USA
Lexington, KY
10 May 2016